The Princess and the Unicorn

Illustrated by Angelika Scudamore
Written by Helen Jones

Brown Watson
ENGLAND
First published 2018 by Brown Watson
The Old Mill, 76 Fleckney Road
Kibworth Beauchamp
Leicestershire LE8 0HG
ISBN: 978 0 7097 2598 5
© 2018 Brown Watson, England
Reprinted 2018
Printed in Malaysia

Princess Lottie was no ordinary princess.
She was brave and strong. She liked archery,
climbing trees and getting muddy.

Most of all she liked riding Sunbeam, her special unicorn. "If only we could go outside the palace grounds," she confided in him one day. "Then I could have a proper adventure."

The Queen was concerned.
"When will she learn to behave like a proper princess?"
she sighed. But the King was rather proud of his daughter.
"That's *my* girl," he said.

One day, a messenger burst into the Royal Dining Room.
"The Dragon has escaped and the people are in danger!"
he declared. "They need your help, Your Majesty."

The King looked grave. "I'm too old for this," he said.
"If only we had a son..." But Princess Lottie stood
up and said, "You don't need a son.
Sunbeam and I will save the people."

"Oh, Lottie!" cried the Queen. "What if you're attacked on route by bandits or bears?" "Not to mention the Dragon himself!" muttered the King.

But Lottie was determined and eventually the King
and Queen agreed to let her go. She packed some food
and her bow and arrows. She mounted Sunbeam
and they set off at top speed.

Before long, Sunbeam and Lottie arrived at a village.
"Look, look!" cried the children and came running out of
their houses. They had never seen a princess before
– or a unicorn for that matter.

The children gathered around them. "Can we ride him?"
asked one little boy. "Does he fly?" asked another.
"No!" laughed Lottie. "He's too young to fly yet.
Sorry... we have to go now."

Sunbeam and Lottie continued on
their way. They entered a large, dark forest.
"Slow down, Sunbeam," said Lottie. "You don't
want to trip over any fallen branches."

Up in the trees, three bear cubs were watching them. "Let's see who the best shot is," said one. "Ready to attack? One, two, three... GO!"

"Ow!" squealed Lottie as a pine cone landed on her head. Suddenly, she and Sunbeam were being pelted with cones. "Stop it!" cried Lottie, looking up. "That hurts.... Oh!"

Lottie had slumped forward. One of the cones had knocked her out! As quick as he could, Sunbeam galloped out of the forest. He found a stream and splashed water on Lottie's wound.

As if by magic, Lottie quickly recovered. "Oh Sunbeam!" she cried. "Thank you for saving me. But we must get on or we'll never rescue the people. Lead the way!"

The path started to climb steeply uphill. It was hot work; the air was still and humid. "That doesn't look good," said Lottie pointing at a dark cloud. "There's a storm ahead."

Before long, the rain was coming down fast.
There was a crack of thunder, and lightning lit up the
whole sky. "Quick! Let's find some shelter," cried Lottie.
But something was wrong. Sunbeam was limping.

What's more, Lottie became aware of
something moving in the valley below. It was big
and green with a swishing tail. "The Dragon!"
she cried. "He's heading for that village!"

"What are we going to do, Sunbeam? Even if you could gallop we'd never make it down there in time." But Sunbeam didn't give up that easily.

With a big whinny, he lifted his legs into the air and suddenly they were flying – over the treetops, over the houses and over a rainbow. "Why, Sunbeam!" exclaimed Lottie. "Now you can fly!"

But her joy was short-lived. The dragon had spotted them and was doing his best to hit them with his massive tail. But Sunbeam quickly dodged out of his way.

Lottie took out her bow and arrows. She focused on her target and fired. The arrow hit the dragon in the neck and he fell to the ground with a big thud.

The villagers ran out of their homes and cheered.
"Long live the Princess! Long live the Princess!"
They fixed Sunbeam's shoe and that evening
they held a big party. Everyone was invited.

"I'm so proud of you," declared the Queen.
"I couldn't agree more," said the King
and winked at Lottie.